HEY ARNOLD! ™

Return of the Sewer King

D0109543

Based on the TV series *Hey Arnold!*® created by
Craig Bartlett as seen on *Nickelodeon*®

No part of this publication may be reproduced in whole or in part, or
stored in a retrieval system, or transmitted in any form or by any
means, electronic, mechanical, photocopying, recording, or
otherwise, without written permission of the publisher.
For information regarding permission, write to Simon Spotlight,
an imprint of Simon & Schuster Children's Publishing Division,
1230 Avenue of the Americas, New York, NY 10020.

ISBN 0-439-23252-X

Copyright © 2000 by Viacom International Inc. All rights reserved.
NICKELODEON, *Hey Arnold!*, and all related titles, logos, and
characters are trademarks of Viacom International Inc. Published by
Scholastic Inc., 555 Broadway, New York, NY 10012,
by arrangement with Simon Spotlight, an imprint of Simon &
Schuster Children's Publishing Division.
SCHOLASTIC and associated logos are trademarks
and/or registered trademarks of Scholastic Inc.

12 11 10 9 8 7 6 5 4 3 2 1   0 1 2 3 4 5/0

Printed in the U.S.A.   40

First Scholastic printing, September 2000

HEY ARNOLD!™

Return of the Sewer King

by **Craig Bartlett**
and **Maggie Groening**
interiors illustrated by
Tim Parsons
cover illustrated by
Tuck Tucker, Kenji Notani,
and **Teale Wang**

SCHOLASTIC INC.
New York   Toronto   London   Auckland   Sydney
Mexico City   New Delhi   Hong Kong

CHAPTER 1

"I'm so *hot*," said Harold. He slumped even lower on Arnold's front stoop.

"We're all hot, Harold. Not a whole lot we can do about it," said Arnold. He sat at the top of the steps holding damp, sticky playing cards. "Go fish," he said to Gerald.

Arnold's friends were gathered on his front stoop. "Used to be when it got this hot, they opened up a fire hydrant for us kids to play in," Stinky whined. "Why not today?"

Sid wiped his forehead and repositioned the backward baseball cap on his head. "There's something weird going on with the water system. It's like the water just disappears for a while every night."

"You got that right," Helga said, scowling. She leaned against the bottom of the stoop banister, her pink hair ribbon looking less perky than usual. "Last night my mom ran the washing machine real late. In the morning the clothes were still full of soap. The machine had quit working in the middle of the job. When she saw it, she gave up and went back to bed."

"How come the water goes off?" asked Harold.

"No one's figured out why," said Gerald.

Just then Grandpa walked up. "What're you kids doing, lying on my stoop like a bunch of three-day-old funeral lilies? Clear the way. You're a fire hazard." He waved a newspaper at them as he trudged up the steps.

Arnold spotted the big headline at the top of the page as Grandpa passed him: "CITY LEADERS STUMPED BY MIDNIGHT WATER STOPPAGE." "Hey, Grandpa, can we borrow your paper?" he asked

"Sure, short man. And then go do something useful. I gotta rinse my dainties before the water goes off again." Grandpa clumped into the boardinghouse and shut the door.

Arnold scanned the newspaper story.

"Anything in that article that explains *why* the water goes off?" asked Gerald, looking over Arnold's shoulder.

"They still don't know," said Arnold. "But it does say the mayor has ordered all city fountains to be turned off."

"Well, that stinks," Helga muttered.

Arnold stood up. "C'mon! Let's go down to the city pool before they close that, too."

Ten minutes later, they stood in front of the city pool, staring at a sweaty city employee posting a newly lettered sign: CITY POOL CLOSED. All of them groaned. "*Closed*?"

"Yeah, closed," the employee grunted. "The mayor says no pools, no fountains, and no fire hydrants, except for emergencies, till they figure out what's going on with the city's water."

The kids trudged back to Arnold's street, where they found several of the neighbors standing outside Mr. Green's butcher shop watching TV, which Mr. Green liked to keep in front of his shop on hot days. Naturally, the neighbors were watching the news about the water shortage. "What do they say, Mr. Green?" Arnold asked.

The butcher turned from the TV and shrugged. "They think there might be some kinda blockage. But they can't explain why the water always goes off exactly at midnight and then comes back on one hour later."

The kids crowded around the TV. Harold wiped some sweat off his brow. "Look, it's Mayor Dixie," he said.

On the TV, Mayor Dixie stood at her official podium, looking tired and cranky. "Our city's water mystery will soon be solved. I've sent for a team of crack water system investigators from the FBI to come and get the job done."

"The FBI? Cool," said Sid.

Mayor Dixie continued. "They are known as the Sewer Gators. They will investigate every foot of pipe until they find the problem and fix it."

"And what do gators have to do with sewers?" Stinky asked.

"It's just a dumb urban legend," Helga snapped. "Some idiots believe that alligators actually live in the sewers of big cities, feeding on rats and garbage, never seeing the light of day."

"Willikers!" Stinky exclaimed, wide-eyed.

Helga snorted, rolling her eyes. "And Arnold's pig can fly, too, Stinko."

"I know it sounds crazy, but it's fun to think about," Arnold said.

"Yeah!" Gerald agreed. "Maybe alligators are behind the water stoppage."

"Alligators? *Please*," Helga said. "I think the heat is getting to all of you."

Arnold ignored Helga. He was suddenly remembering something. He turned to Gerald. "I don't see how alligators could be responsible for this, Gerald. But I know a certain sewer resident that *could* be."

The two exchanged a glance that was full of meaning.

"The Sewer King!" breathed Gerald. "Of course!"

CHAPTER 2

"The *what* king?" asked Helga. No one could believe their ears.

Gerald hesitated. "I . . . ah, forget about it."

"Aw, come on, tell us!" Harold insisted.

"Tell us, Gerald. As Keeper of Urban Legends, it is your sacred duty," Sid said.

"Well, I can," Gerald said, glancing at Arnold, "but it's no legend. This actually happened to Arnold and me."

Stinky and Sid leaned in closer.

"We've never told anyone before, 'cause we didn't think anyone would believe us," added Arnold.

"Oh, cut the suspense and just get on with it," said Helga.

Arnold slowly nodded to Gerald, who stood up and cleared his throat. "Once, not too long ago," he began, "Arnold and I descended into the sewers. We were looking for his grandpa's watch. What we found was a huge tunnel system with streams and rivers going in all directions. Darkness. Rats. And the smell? HoooooEEE! We found the watch . . . and much more. We also found . . . the Sewer King!"

"The Sewer King, huh? Who elected him king? The cockroaches?" sneered Helga.

"He appointed himself, I guess," Gerald said. "Anyway, he lives down there. He rules over the rats and the cockroaches. He *never*

comes out. He was planning to keep Arnold and me as his Royal Rat Groomers. He almost kept us, too. Right, Arnold?"

"Right," Arnold said. "Only we made it to a sewer opening just in the nick of time. When we got the lid open and the Sewer King saw the sunlight, he let out this awful scream and ran away."

"Back down to the depths of his underground kingdom, never to be heard from again," finished Gerald.

"Unless . . ." said Arnold. He looked at Gerald.

"Unless, *he's* the one who's behind the stopped-up water problem," Gerald said slowly.

"I'm confused, fellers. Yer sayin' it *ain't* alligators?" Stinky asked.

A great sob suddenly escaped from Harold. "Please don't talk about alligators anymore! *Please!*" he cried.

"Oh, what now, you big baby?" Helga rolled her eyes. "There aren't any alligators in the sewer—it's just a story."

"I'm *not* afraid of alligators! It's just . . . it's . . . it's . . . oh, Stubby! My little Stubby!" Harold burst into a fresh flood of tears.

Arnold turned to Sid. "What's he talking about?"

"A pet alligator he used to have," said Sid, speaking loudly so that he could be heard over Harold's sobbing.

"My uncle Stanley—he lives in Florida and he runs an alligator farm there—he sent me Stubby a coupla years ago," Harold said, sobbing.

"He was about six inches long. And he had a little stub for a tail," added Sid.

"Exactly six inches! I used to measure him with my ruler." Harold brightened a little at the memory. "My uncle couldn't use him for the farm with his stubby tail, so he let me have him. I fed him little pieces of hamburger. He knew his name. He came when I called him. He loved to have his belly rubbed. I'd yell, 'Roll over for a tummy rub, Stubby!' and he'd roll right over. . . .' " Harold's face crumpled, and he burst into fresh tears.

"What happened to him, Harold?" Arnold gently asked. But Harold couldn't answer Arnold, he was sobbing so hard.

"Harold took Stubby for a swim in the big fountain at the park. Stubby went under the water and never came up again," Sid finished for him.

Helga waved her arm, annoyed. "All right, enough alligator stories. What about your Sewer King?" she demanded of Arnold and Gerald. "Are you losers gonna find out what he knows about the water stoppage?"

Gerald shook his head. "I don't think that's a good idea. That dude is dangerous."

"We'd better try to find him," said Arnold quietly.

"What?" Gerald yelped.

"If anyone knows what's going on with the city's water, it's him, Gerald. Besides, with those FBI guys coming, he could be in big trouble."

Helga smirked. "Go on, football head. Find your mythical Sewer King for us. Before we all dry up and blow away."

Arnold looked at Gerald and asked, "Tonight at midnight?"

Gerald gave him a weak smile. "Okay, but I've got a feeling I'm gonna regret this."

CHAPTER 3

Late that night, Gerald knocked three times and let himself into Arnold's attic room.

"You brought the map. Great." Arnold took it from Gerald and spread it out on his bed.

Gerald looked uncomfortable. "Yeah, but, uh . . . I was thinking maybe we should rethink this whole thing."

"Rethink what?"

"Arnold, I don't think that map is going to

be much help if we need to make a quick exit. Especially if that weird guy chases us again. He was *totally* creepy, remember? Why do we want to go *looking* for him?"

"To solve the mystery, Gerald. So the fountains and the hydrants can be turned on again."

"Oh, yeah." Gerald looked unconvinced.

"So my grandpa doesn't have to go to bed with his hands stuck together because there was no water to wash with," Arnold continued.

"Stuck together?"

"He was putting up wallpaper."

"At midnight?"

"Yeah, well. You know Grandpa. And Gerald, I've been thinking about Sam. I'm worried about him."

"Sam?"

"You know, the Sewer King."

Gerald rolled his eyes. "I didn't realize you two were on a first-name basis."

"I hate to think what might happen to him if those FBI Sewer Gator guys find him. We ought to at least warn him, so he can hide or something."

"Arnold, it's real hard for me to feel worried about a lunatic who was ready to draft me as permanent Royal Rat Groomer."

"I know he's nuts, Gerald. But he needs help. Obviously he has no one. And this time, *we* need *his* help too."

Gerald sighed. "Okay, okay, I'll do it. Let's just get it over with."

They surveyed the equipment spread out on Arnold's bed: two flashlights, a map, Gerald's watch, and a ball of string.

Gerald poked the string. "What's this for?"

"To mark our path. We tie one end near where we go in. Then we unwind the string as we go. That way, we can follow the string all the way back when we're done."

"I'm looking forward to that part," said Gerald. Together they put the supplies into their pockets.

"Almost midnight, Arnold."

"Okay, let's go."

Arnold and Gerald tiptoed down the stairs. Slowly and carefully they opened the creaking front door. They looked around the deserted street.

"Where do we go in?" asked Gerald.

Arnold pointed to a manhole cover with a recessed handle. "I already looked in—there's a ladder inside that goes straight down."

They pried open the cover and slid it over to expose the tunnel. They peered down inside.

"It's really dark down there, Arnold."

"That's why we've got flashlights, Gerald."

Arnold lowered his feet onto the ladder and started climbing down. After just a few steps Gerald couldn't see him anymore. But he could hear Arnold's feet on the iron rungs that were set into the wall.

Then the footsteps stopped.

"You coming, Gerald?" Arnold called.

"Yeah, I'm coming, I'm coming," Gerald said.

And he, too, started down the ladder into the darkness.

CHAPTER 4

The ladder seemed endless, but Arnold's foot finally touched solid ground beneath the final rung. He turned and shone his flashlight into the darkness. Ahead was a large, round, stone-lined tunnel with a stream of dark water flowing down its center. There were other tunnels branching off from it in the distance. Arnold tied one end of the string to the ladder and whispered up to Gerald, "You okay?"

"Yeah, yeah! Keep your shirt on," Gerald grumbled as he jumped off the last rung. He sighed. "Let's get this over with, Arnold."

"Okay. Just don't trip on the string."

They started off down the tunnel, walking on either side of the stream. Gerald ran his flashlight beam over the walls and ceiling as they walked. "Hey, Arnold? I keep seeing little eyes looking at us, and when I look again, they're gone."

"It's probably your imagination, Gerald. Or else it's just the rats."

"Oh, yeah. Just the rats." Gerald shifted over to Arnold's side of the stream.

They walked on. The smell in the tunnel was nasty, and the air was thick and still.

"Hey, Arnold? You think this stream is getting narrower, or is that my imagination too?"

"No, you're right. It *is* getting narrower.

And the water is moving slower than it was. I wonder what that means."

As they walked along, the water slowed to a trickle and stopped. Up ahead, Arnold and Gerald could see a large opening in the tunnel. There was a dimly lit open space on the other side. As they approached they heard the sound of water sloshing against stone walls.

Gerald checked his watch. It was almost one o'clock in the morning. He showed the time to Arnold, who nodded and put his finger to his lips. They turned off their flashlights, crept up to the opening, and peered in.

In front of them was a huge underground chamber with high, stone-lined ceilings and arches. The room was completely flooded with inky water that flowed into a giant, black pool. Arnold and Gerald watched the water, noticing little waves and ripples moving over its surface.

"Hey, Arnold? Why is the water down there moving so much?"

"Maybe there's a current. Gerald, look at the water level. It looks like it's going down."

"And fast! See? It's running out that tunnel over there." Gerald pointed to the far side of the pool, where water was rushing into a large tunnel like the one they had just come out of. Then they noticed a movement on that side, and spotted a large human shape standing by another tunnel opening. It wore a hard hat with a headlamp on it, a long, flowing cape, and held a stick that looked like a toilet plunger.

"The Sewer King!" Arnold whispered.

CHAPTER 5

"It *is* the Sewer King! What's he doing?" asked Gerald.

He seemed to be watching the pool near his feet. In the darkness Gerald and Arnold could make out some dark shapes of animals climbing out of the water and going down the tunnel next to him.

The Sewer King spoke to them as they went by. "Very good, my lovelies. You must be hungry. Time to return to the royal chambers."

And then suddenly he was gone, his cape sweeping after him as he disappeared down the tunnel.

Gerald and Arnold couldn't move until the water stopped draining out of the enormous pool and its surface settled to an oily smoothness.

"The water's stopped draining. Let's follow him," Arnold said.

"What, are you crazy? There's no *way* to get over to that tunnel he went down."

"I bet we could cross the pool now," said Arnold. "It looks like it might be pretty shallow."

"I am *not* stepping into that water. Who knows how deep it is?"

"Well, what are we going to do? We found Sam! Now we need to go talk to him."

"We found him, Arnold, but then we lost him. We'll just have to come back a little earlier next time, and try to talk to him when he comes to this room again."

"Maybe you're right. At least we've figured out where to find him between midnight and one o'clock."

"Great, Arnold! Mission accomplished. Now let's get out of here."

"Okay. We'll come back tomorrow night. I think I would prefer talking to Sam from this side of the water, anyway," Arnold said.

But he might as well have said it to himself, because Gerald was already rolling up the string and heading back down the tunnel.

CHAPTER 6

The next night, Arnold and Gerald met at the same sewer entrance and headed down the hole again. The smell in the tunnel was even stronger this time. The little stream down the middle was slow and shallow as they began their underground walk. This time, Gerald didn't shine his flashlight around to look at the walls. They needed to get to the big chamber quickly.

As they hurried along, Arnold suddenly

realized that his feet were wet. He looked down at the floor. "Gerald? Is the stream getting wider this time?"

Gerald looked down. "Yeah. There's less dry floor for walking on. And it's moving faster."

They kept going. The water kept rising. Soon they were ankle-deep, and then knee-deep in the dark, rushing water.

"Arnold, I *really* hate this."

"Come on, Gerald—we're almost there." Ahead of them was the opening in the tunnel that led to the big room.

Suddenly, they heard a loud gushing sound behind them. They turned and saw a huge, roaring flood of water! It filled the tunnel almost to the ceiling. Arnold and Gerald were swept off their feet in the powerful current, and then tossed down underwater! They kicked and clawed back to

the surface, sputtering and choking. There was nothing to hang on to to stop them from being carried along right to the chamber entrance. They washed over the edge in a huge waterfall, down into the pool below.

For several terrifying seconds, the two boys struggled to get out from under the pounding waterfall that kept forcing them underwater. Finally they swam down and back toward the wall, and came up directly behind the waterfall. They clung to the stones with white knuckles, gasping for air.

"Gerald—you okay?" Arnold choked as he spit out a mouthful of water.

"I'm doing great, Arnold. I always wondered how it felt to get flushed down a toilet."

"Good. Hang on to the wall here. I think this is a good place to hide while we wait for Sam."

"Oh, just what I was thinking. No one would ever expect intruders to hide in sewer water, so we're perfectly safe." Gerald rolled his eyes.

Arnold let go of the wall with one hand to push the wet hair off his face, when something caught his eye. "Look—there he is!"

Arnold and Gerald edged over to peek around one side of the waterfall, which suddenly wasn't as strong. The Sewer King was looking into the pool from his tunnel entrance across the way. He watched the dark swimming shapes in the pool with a satisfied smile. Arnold and Gerald could see his lips moving, but they couldn't hear him over the sound of the waterfall.

"I never signed on for swimming with rats, Arnold," said Gerald with a whimper. "Can we please get out of here?"

"Sorry, Gerald, we're stuck for now. Unless you're ready to swim across to Sam and ask him to pull us out."

"That's okay. I'll wait." Gerald moved closer against the wall and adjusted his grip.

They clung there for what seemed like forever, watching the Sewer King and nervously keeping track of the movements of the swimming shapes around them. Just when it seemed like they couldn't hang on to the slippery, cold stones another minute, one of the creatures surfaced directly in front of Arnold and gazed at him with cold, yellow eyes.

"Umm, Gerald?" Arnold gasped.

"Yeah?"

"I don't think these are rats."

"Why not?" Gerald asked, hanging on for dear life.

"Aren't rats supposed to have ears?"

"Usually . . ."

"And whiskers, and fur?"

"What are you getting at, Arnold?"

"Don't panic, Gerald . . . but these aren't rats, they're *alligators*!"

CHAPTER 7

"*Alligators?!*" Gerald screamed. "*Agghhhhhh! Get me out of here! Help!*" He splashed wildly against the wall.

The Sewer King looked up in alarm at the commotion by the waterfall. Then he hurried to usher his alligators out of the pool and down the tunnel.

"Come on, my beauties, my loyal subjects. Quickly, quickly! The kingdom is under attack!" He dashed down the tunnel behind the last of his obedient reptiles.

Suddenly the exit tunnel across the pool opened wide. Water began rushing out of the pool. Gerald was quickly swept away from the wall and got caught in the rapid current. He was heading right toward the tunnel. Arnold hung on for a moment longer. But when Gerald disappeared in the flood, he let go and allowed himself to be carried into the tunnel too.

It was a wild ride down the twisting, rushing tunnel. The water was fast and furious. Arnold and Gerald both went under more than once and came up gasping and choking as they were swept along.

Then the tunnel widened very abruptly, and the water slowed down and deposited the two boys on a wide, sloping ledge of slick concrete. They lay there for a few seconds, sputtering and stunned.

"What do you want here? I *command* you to explain yourselves!" roared a voice behind them. The voice echoed wildly against the walls of the large underground room.

Arnold and Gerald looked up and saw the Sewer King, seated on his throne—a spectacular, gleaming toilet—wielding his plunger and fixing them with a furious glare. His wide, soft face was the same bluish white they remembered from their last meeting.

Arnold pulled himself painfully to his feet, water still pouring off of him.

"Uh, Your Majesty? We're here to bring you some news from . . . the land above. And to find some answers," Arnold began.

The Sewer King scowled.

Arnold hurried on. "First of all, why are you turning the water off for an hour every night?"

"The Prince of the Pipes does not answer

questions! He *asks* them! And if he doesn't like your answers, he feeds you incompetent villains to his Royal Guards!" The Sewer King gestured grandly, and Arnold and Gerald noticed several alligators of various sizes lying limply around him.

"As it happens, my guards are hungry. They have just had their regular swim in the pool I created. Exercise keeps them in top condition."

"I should have known. If there *are* alligators in the sewer, this weirdo would be behind it," Gerald muttered.

"So you turn off the city's water so your alligators can swim each night? But you can't keep doing that. The people above are angry. If you don't stop, they will make you stop," Arnold said.

"But I have to give my darlings their swim. It keeps them well. I have rescued each and every one of them from the cold and uncaring Surface Dwellers. Thoughtlessly buying alligators as tiny, pretty pets, they flush them down to me when they grow weary of their snapping ways."

The Sewer King gazed down at his motionless reptiles. "I have nursed my splendid army of alligators back to health. I have fed and cared for them and have exercised them down here in my kingdom of the depths. And now they work for me," he crooned.

Then he fixed the boys with a fierce glare. "So get out. Your threats mean nothing to me."

Arnold and Gerald looked at each other in dismay. This was not going to be easy. But Arnold had an idea.

CHAPTER 8

"Sam . . . ," Arnold began.

The Sewer King looked up angrily.

"Your Highness, I mean," added Arnold. "You can't do this anymore. The mayor is sending the FBI down here to your kingdom. You will be found, and they will take you away—*to the surface*."

The Sewer King recoiled as if struck.

Arnold continued, "You have to stop turning off the water *now*. That's the only way to keep them from investigating," he explained.

"But my beauties must have their swim! Before I made the pool for them, they were sluggish and ill. If I take it away from them, my noble guards will wither and wilt!" cried the Sewer King in anguish.

"Frankly, they're not looking so great as it is," said Gerald.

It was true. The alligators looked dull, sad, and tired. The Sewer King looked around at them, his face suddenly full of grief.

"And what about you?" asked Arnold. "This can't be such a great place for a human being to live."

"I am no ordinary human being!" roared the Sewer King.

"Of course not," Arnold added. "But, Sam, it's horrible down here. It's filthy and smelly and disgusting. . . ."

"Not to mention unsanitary," said Gerald.

"That's where you're *wrong!*" roared the Sewer King. "Yes, there is a certain odor associated with sewer life, but I have all the comforts of you Surface Dwellers, *and* all without ever exposing myself to . . . *the light.*" He crossed over to a very large pipe that was attached to the wall.

"Behold! I partake of a warm, soapy shower every day"—he turned a valve, and sudsy water poured out of an opening in the side of the pipe—"courtesy of my clever wiring of the waste water pipe from *your* Sir Suds-a-Lot!"

"Sir Suds-a-Lot?" Gerald asked, looking at Arnold.

"You know, the laundromat on Forty-fifth Street," whispered Arnold.

"That's great, Your Highness, really. But what about the alligators? I mean, *look* at them."

"Enough! I will not listen to your foolish yapping anymore!" He closed the valve, and the soapy water stopped flowing.

"Courtiers, summon the Mighty Gigantor, my finest champion! It is time to attack! *Gigantor!*"

Arnold and Gerald glanced at each other nervously, then eyed the alligators on the floor. They wondered which one was the champion.

Suddenly, the huge pipe that contained Sam's shower began to rumble and shake. The Sewer King ran to the end of the pipe and swung open a great hatchway.

A giant alligator, its head more than twice as big as any of the others', appeared at the opening, filling the entire pipe.

"Seize them, Gigantor, seize them!" screamed the Sewer King, dancing with delight.

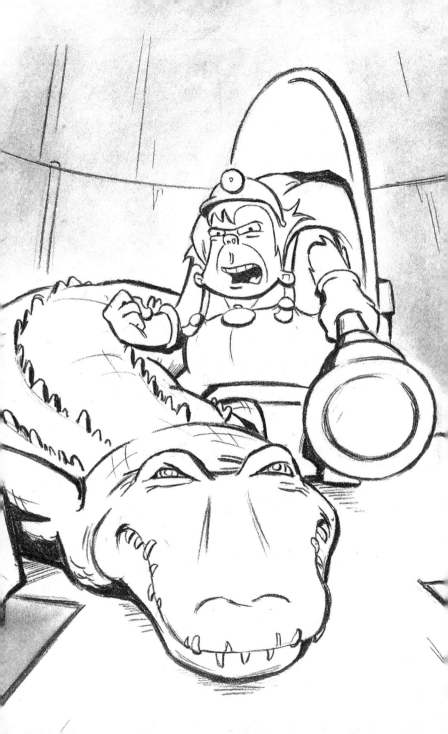

The huge alligator slipped to the floor and lurched toward the boys. His eyes were cold, and his teeth were huge. Arnold and Gerald looked wildly around, searching for somewhere to run. But there was no way out!

CHAPTER 9

Arnold looked at the twelve-foot alligator quickly closing in on them. Then he noticed something. "Stubby?!" he murmured to himself.

"What?!" yelped Gerald.

"Gerald, look at his tail! It's Harold's Stubby!"

Gerald looked. The alligator did have a short stump of a tail, much shorter than those of the other alligators'. "But, Arnold, Stubby is six inches long!" Gerald screamed.

"Stubby *was* six inches long, but that was a couple of years ago!" Arnold yelled back. He called out to the giant alligator lumbering toward them. "Stubby?"

Gerald joined in. "Nice Stubby!"

The alligator stood very still for a moment. He blinked, confused.

The Sewer King's eyes bulged. He was furious. Why didn't his prize gator attack?

Arnold and Gerald stood there, tense. Finally Arnold crouched down on his knees and said, "Stubby, how you been?"

The alligator slowly rolled over onto his back. Arnold began rubbing his belly. Stubby groaned sadly.

"Look, Sewer King. This alligator is not happy. He needs to live where other alligators live. Aboveground! They all do," Arnold said.

The Sewer King wrung his hands unhappily. He knew Arnold was right. "I know, I know! I've done everything I can, but it's not enough! Oh, how can I help my lovelies!"

Arnold, still petting Stubby, glanced at Gerald. "Well, there's always Harold's uncle's alligator farm. Do you think he might be willing to take in a bunch of fine specimens like these?" Arnold asked.

"Good idea, Arnold. Or at least he'll know what to do with them."

They looked over at the Sewer King. He was hunched on his throne, his face in his hands.

"What about you, Your Highness?"

The Sewer King lifted his tear-streaked face. "You may have my Royal Guards. I know it is best for them. But you will *never* take me. My loyal rats and I will remain here in my kingdom. I could never consent to venture to"—he shuddered—"the surface. And who knows? Perhaps with the Royal Guards in exile, the rats will become less skittish." He smiled sadly.

"Okay, Sewer King. We'll make a deal with you: You let us help the alligators, and you quit shutting off the water every night," said Arnold.

"No need for that anymore," muttered the Sewer King.

"And we won't tell the Surface Dwellers about you and your kingdom. Just quit messing with the water supply, okay? It's *hot* up there."

CHAPTER 10

The next day, Arnold and Gerald enjoyed being able to tell Harold the news that his little Stubby had been found. It was even more fun when Harold saw how huge he had become.

As they had agreed, the Sewer King led all the alligators to a prearranged meeting place: a pond near the city's sewage treatment plant. Harold's uncle brought his big truck, collected all the alligators, and transported them to his farm in Florida. And he took Harold with him to see them installed in their new home.

One hot day, late that summer, Arnold, Gerald, and several of the other kids gathered to cool their feet in the sparkling fountain in the park.

"Hey, you guys! I'm back!" yelled Harold, hurrying over. "Florida was cool! The alligators are doing great! And Stubby is the star of the whole place!" He beamed. "I'm so proud!"

He grinned at Arnold, who was wading around in the fountain's basin. "Thanks a lot, Arnold. You did a great thing, saving Stubby like that."

He turned to Gerald. "You too, Gerald. I love you guys." Harold noticed that Gerald was sitting far away from the fountain's edge,

and that his shoes and socks were still on. "Hey. Why aren't you in there with everyone else? It's *hot*!" Harold asked.

Gerald eyed the pool doubtfully. "I don't know—I'm just kinda nervous about it. Ever since swimming with those alligators . . ."

"Come on, Gerald. There aren't any alligators in the sewer anymore. That's just a myth, remember?" said Arnold.

Gerald began to take off his shoes. "Yeah, you're right—it *is* just a myth, thanks to us. But next time you wanna go visit the Sewer King, Arnold . . . take Helga with you, okay?"

about the authors

Hey Arnold! creator Craig Bartlett was born in Seattle, Washington. He wanted to grow up to be either an artist or a secret agent, but became an animator instead. He moved to Los Angeles in 1987 to direct the Penny cartoons for *PeeWee's Playhouse.* Craig stayed to write and direct on the first season of *Rugrats,* which introduced him to his friends at Nickelodeon. He premiered his first episode of *Hey Arnold!* on Nick in 1996, and has since made 100 episodes. He lives with his wife, Lisa, and kids, Matt and Katie, in Glendale, California, and enjoys painting, snorkeling, and reading the *New Yorker* magazine, preferably in Hawaii.

Maggie Groening was born in Portland, Oregon, where she grew up wanting to be a writer and watching a lot of TV. She moved to New York City in 1983, and worked as a writer for Children's Television Workshop, Disney, and many textbook companies. In 1991 she wrote the Maggie Simpson book series with her brother and coauthor Matt Groening. She lives in Brooklyn, New York, with her husband, Potter; her children, Franklin and Louise; and a crabby cat.

YOU CAN ENTER FOR A CHANCE TO **WIN A TRIP** FOR FOUR TO **NICKELODEON STUDIOS® FLORIDA!**

1 GRAND PRIZE:
A 3-day/2-night trip for four to Nickelodeon Studios in Orlando, Florida

3 FIRST PRIZES:
A Sony Playstation® system and a *Rugrats™ in Paris* Playstation game from THQ®

25 SECOND PRIZES:
A *The Wild Thornberrys* CD-ROM from Mattel Interactive

100 THIRD PRIZES:
A set of four books from Simon & Schuster Children's Publishing, including a *The Wild Thornberrys* title, a *Rugrats* title, a *SpongeBob SquarePants* title, and a *Hey Arnold!* title

Complete entry form and send to:
Simon & Schuster Children's Publishing Division
Marketing Department/ "Nickelodeon Studios Florida Sweepstakes"
1230 Avenue of the Americas, 4th Floor, NY, NY 10020

Name_____ Birthdate___/___/_____

Address_____

City_____ State_____ Zip_____

Phone (____) _____

Parent/Guardian Signature _____

See back for official rules.

Simon & Schuster Children's Publishing Division/ "Nickelodeon Studios Florida Sweepstakes" Sponsor's Official Rules:

NO PURCHASE NECESSARY.

Enter by mailing this completed Official Entry Form (no copies allowed) or by mailing a 3 1/2" x 5" card with your complete name and address, parent and/or legal guardian's name, daytime telephone number, and birthdate to the Simon & Schuster Children's Publishing Division/ "Nickelodeon Studios Florida Sweepstakes," 1230 Avenue of the Americas, 4th Floor, NY, NY 10020. Entry forms are available in the back of *The Rugrats Files #3: The Quest for the Holey Pail* (12/2000), *Rugrats Chapter Book #10: Dil in a Pickle* (11/2000), *The Wild Thornberrys Chapter Book #2: Two Promises Too Many!* (9/2000), *The Wild Thornberrys Chapter Book #3: A Time to Share* (9/2000), *SpongeBob SquarePants Trivia Book* (9/2000), *SpongeBob SquarePants Joke Book* (9/2000), *Hey Arnold! Chapter Book #1: Arnold for President* (9/2000), and *Hey Arnold! Chapter Book #2: Return of the Sewer King* (9/2000), and on the web site SimonSaysKids.com. Sweepstakes begins 8/1/2000 and ends 2/28/2001. Entries must be postmarked by 2/28/01 and received by 3/15/01. Not responsible for lost, late, damaged, postage-due, stolen, illegible, mutilated, incomplete, or misdirected or not delivered entries or mail, or for typographical errors in the entry form or rules. Entries are void if they are in whole or in part illegible, incomplete, or damaged. Enter as often as you wish, but each entry must be mailed separately. Entries will not be returned. Winners will be selected at random from all eligible entries received in a drawing to be held on or about 3/30/01. Grand prize winner must be available to travel during the months of June and July 2001. If Grand Prize winner is unable to travel on the specified dates, prize will be forfeited and awarded to an alternate. Winners will be notified by mail within 30 days of selection. The grand prize winner will be notified by phone as well. Odds of winning depend on the number of eligible entries received.

Prizes: One Grand Prize: A 3-day/2-night trip for four to Nickelodeon Studios in Orlando, FL, including a VIP tour, admission for four to Universal Studios Florida, round-trip coach airfare from a major U.S. airport nearest the winner's residence, and standard hotel accommodations (2 rooms, double occupancy) of sponsor's choice. (Total approx. retail value: $2,700.00). Winner must be accompanied by a parent or legal guardian. Prize does not include transfers, gratuities, or any other expenses not specified or listed herein. 3 First Prizes: A Sony Playstation system and a *Rugrats* Playstation game from THQ. (Total approx. retail value: $150.00 each). 25 Second Prizes: A *The Wild Thornberrys* CD-ROM from Mattel Interactive. (Approx. retail value: $29.99 each). 100 Third Prizes: A set of four books from Simon & Schuster Children's Publishing, including a *The Wild Thornberrys* title, a *Rugrats* title, a *SpongeBob SquarePants* title, and a *Hey Arnold!* title. (Total approx. retail value: $12.00 per set).

The sweepstakes is open to legal residents of the continental U.S. (excluding Puerto Rico) and Canada (excluding Quebec) ages 5-13 as of 2/28/01. Proof of age is required to claim prize. Prizes will be awarded to winner's parent or legal guardian. Void wherever prohibited or restricted by law. All provincial, federal, state, and local laws apply. Simon & Schuster Inc. and MTV Networks and their respective officers, directors, shareholders, employees, suppliers, parent companies, subsidiaries, affiliates, agencies, sponsors, participating retailers, and persons connected with the use, marketing, or conducting of this sweepstakes are not eligible. Family members living in the same household as any of the individuals referred to in the preceding sentence are not eligible.

One prize per person or household. Prizes are not transferable, have no cash equivalent, and may not be substituted except by sponsors, in the event of prize unavailability, in which case a prize of equal or greater value will be awarded. All prizes will be awarded.

If a winner is a Canadian resident, then he/she must correctly answer a skill-based question administered by mail.

All expenses on receipt and use of prize including provincial, federal, state, and local taxes are the sole responsibility of the winner's parent or legal guardian. Winners' parents or legal guardians may be required to execute and return an Affidavit of Eligibility and Publicity Release and all other legal documents which the sweepstakes sponsors may require (including a W-9 tax form) within 15 days of attempted notification or an alternate winner will be selected. The grand prize winner, parent or legal guardian, and travel companions will be required to execute a liability release form prior to ticketing.

Winners' parents or legal guardians on behalf of the winners agree to allow use of winners' names, photographs, likenesses, and entries for any advertising, promotion, and publicity purposes without further compensation to or permission from the entrants, except where prohibited by law.

Winners and winners' parents or legal guardians agree that Simon & Schuster, Inc., Nickelodeon Studios, THQ, and MTV Networks and their respective officers, directors, shareholders, employees, suppliers, parent companies, subsidiaries, affiliates, agencies, sponsors, participating retailers, and persons connected with the use, marketing, or conducting of this sweepstakes shall have no responsibility or liability for injuries, losses, or damages of any kind in connection with the collection, acceptance, or use of the prizes awarded herein, or from participation in this promotion.

By participating in this sweepstakes, entrants agree to be bound by these rules and the decisions of the judges and sweepstakes sponsors, which are final in all matters relating to the sweepstakes. Failure to comply with the Official Rules may result in a disqualification of your entry and prohibition of any further participation in this sweepstakes.

The first names of the winners will be posted at SimonSaysKids.com or the first names of the winners may be obtained by sending a stamped, self-addressed envelope after 3/30/01 to Prize Winners, Simon & Schuster Children's Publishing Division "Nickelodeon Studios Sweepstakes," 1230 Avenue of the Americas, 4th Floor, NY, NY 10020.

Sponsor of sweepstakes is Simon & Schuster Inc.

© 2000 Viacom International Inc. All Rights Reserved. Nickelodeon and all related titles, characters, and logos are trademarks of Viacom International Inc.